What Shall We Do With The **BOO HOO BABY?**

For perplexed parents everywhere - C.C.

First published in 2000 by Macmillan Children's Books
A division of Macmillan Publishers Limited
25 Eccleston Place, London SW1W 9NF
Basingstoke and Oxford
Associated companies throughout the world
www.panmacmillan.com

ISBN 0 333 73592 7 HB
ISBN 0 333 73593 5 PB

3 5 7 9 8 6 4 2

A CIP catalogue record for this book is available from the British Library.

Printed in Belgium by Proost.

What Shall We Do With The BOO HOO BABY?

by Cressida Cowell

Illustrated by Ingrid Godon

MACMILLAN CHILDREN'S BOOKS

The baby said,

What shall we do with
the boo-hoo baby?

"Feed him," said the dog.

So they fed the baby.

"Miaow!" said the cat.

"Boo-hoo-hoo!"

said the baby.

What shall we do with the boo-hoo baby?

"Play with him," said the cow.

So they played with the baby.

"Boo-hoo-hoo!"

said the baby.

What shall we do with the boo-hoo baby?

"Put him to bed," said the duck.

"Miaow!" said the cat.

So they put him to bed.

"Bow-wow!" said the dog.

"Quack!" said the duck.

"Moo!" said the cow,

and . . .

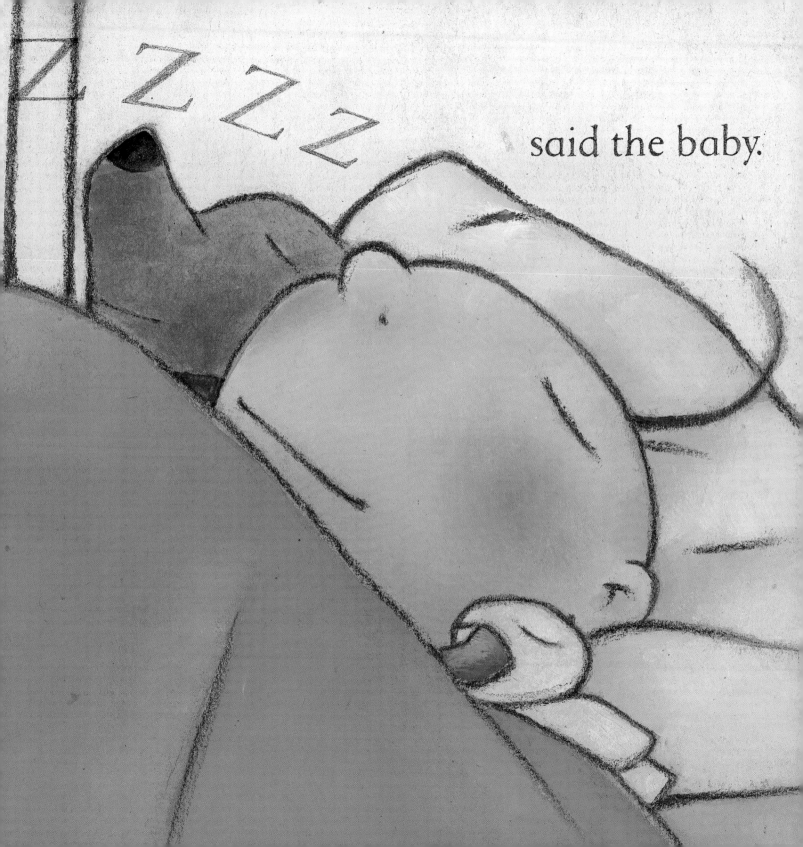

ZZZZZ

said the baby.